Across a Stream

CHARACTERS

Narrator 1

Talking Feather

Narrator 2

Melissa Johnson

Henry Johnson

Wild Tooth

SETTING

Montana, early 1800s

Narrator 1: In the early 1800s, there was a rush to settle lands west of the Mississippi River, in a place now called Montana. Those lands were already inhabited by Native Americans who had lived there for many years before the settlers arrived.

Talking Feather: I am called Talking Feather. I am a Lemhi Shoshone. My people used to live on the plains of what will be called Montana, but now we live in the Rocky Mountains and westward to the Salmon River. I am the wife of Wild Tooth. We have one son.

Narrator 2: Settlers came from all over. They were young and old. They traveled hundreds of miles in all sorts of weather in pursuit of land and a new life.

Melissa Johnson: My name is Melissa Johnson. I was born in Kettlesburg, Illinois. When I was 10, I moved west with my family. My father was a farmer, and we lived in a sod hut. When I was 18, I married Henry Johnson. I knew him only a short time, having met him on his way to homestead in the Montana territories. Two weeks after we met, we got married. The very next day, we began the long wagon journey to our new home.

Henry Johnson: My name is Henry Johnson. I'm a farmer, or at least I am a farmer now. I used to be a printer in Joplin, Missouri. My dad was a printer, as was his dad. But I had a desire to move on. I didn't want to stay in Joplin anymore. There was a notice from the territorial government of Montana that any able-bodied man could claim 100 acres of prime farming land. The land would be his if he survived five years and built a home, a barn, and such. I didn't know much about farming, but I was willing to learn. I sold my presses and bought a wagon, a mule, and supplies to get me started.

Wild Tooth: I am Wild Tooth, a hunter and a warrior in the Shoshone tribe. I am married to Talking Feather. We have a son who will follow in my footsteps. My father is Kind Heart, the tribal medicine man. I was to become a medicine man, too, but my shadow was that of a hunter. My younger brother now follows in my father's footsteps. Our tribe has traveled to the land of the big sky to hunt and fish as we have every spring for all our history.

Narrator 1: The Shoshone were nomadic, moving down from the mountains to the vast plains as their needs required. They hadn't been to this particular big sky campsite for many years. When they got there, they saw that much had changed, including who now lived there.

Talking Feather: In all my life, I had never seen a white man, although I had heard many campfire stories about him. What I had heard and what I saw were very different. I was taught to fear the white man. The stories told that he was mean as a wolverine and smelled of smoke and grease. When we reached the big sky, I was surprised by what I saw.

Melissa Johnson: We barely survived our first winter. Henry had built a log cabin, but it was small and the winter was long and bitter. The snows finally melted, and the spring flowers bloomed. I thought our worries were over, but then the Indians camped on our land. I was frightened by these strangers.

Narrator 2: The Shoshone had their way of life, as did the settlers. Now those ways of life were about to confront each other.

Wild Tooth: The white man was where he should not be. While we were gone, he had chopped down a forest I knew as a child. In its place he had built a log cabin. Now he was cutting up the earth by pulling wooden stakes with a horse. Nervously, we set up our teepees in the place of our ancestors.

Henry Johnson: I was plowing at the time. Bessie-Belle, my mule, was leaning into the leather harness when I looked up and saw them at the edge of the clearing. I fetched my gun from the cabin and told Melissa to stay inside. I had heard stories about the Indians, and I was afraid for my family.

Narrator 1: The Shoshone tribe put up their teepees and went about their daily lives. The women and children collected water from the streams in tanned leather bags. The men and older boys hobbled the horses with leather thongs that they tied between the horses' front legs.

Narrator 2: The settlers cleared the land, planted crops, and built houses.

Talking Feather: Strangers living on our land spoiled our happiness at being back at the big sky. The white man had chopped down a grove of trees and with it the summer choke-cherries I loved to pick as a child.

Narrator 2: The Shoshone lamented the changes that the settlers' actions had brought.

Talking Feather: Still, the stream water was sweet, and we could see fish playing in the shadows of the rocks.

Melissa Johnson: I pulled a chunk of moss from between the logs and watched the Indians set up camp. In the meadow near the stream, they erected their tents made of animal skins. One moment the field was empty; the next moment there was a village of tents, with cook fires blazing and children running about. These people don't seem as fearsome as I imagined. I put the baby back in his rocker and went about cooking venison stew for supper.

Narrator 1: Aware of each other's presence, the women went about their chores.

Henry Johnson: I stood there for a while, the buffalo gun cradled in my arms. I was sure the Indians could see that I was armed and figured it was best not to attack us. Melissa had gone about her chores as if nothing was wrong. But I was troubled.

Wild Tooth: The white man stood with his long gun and stared at us. I was comforted by the knife strapped to my waist. My longbow and stone-tipped arrows in their quiver were never out of my sight. I was alert and prepared.

Narrator 2: Day turned to dusk, and dusk to night as the standoff continued. Dead wood gathered from the forest floor was added to the cook fire.

Narrator 1: Several rabbits and wild game birds began to roast over the flames of the Indian encampment. Smoke from the cabin snaked into a darkening sky.

Melissa Johnson: As the afternoon dragged on, I forgot about the Indians. Using the last of the peaches my mother had preserved for our journey, I baked a pie for Henry. He had stood outside all day and gotten nothing done. Just before the Sun set, he went to the corral, haltered Bessie-Belle, and pulled her, braying, up close to the house. He tied her to the porch support. She wasn't at all happy.

Talking Feather: Using snares, some of the boys caught rabbits that were quickly skinned. Their hides were pulled tight over willow frames and set out to cure. The meat was put over the fire as I dug in the underbrush for wild onion to season the meat. Settling in, I forgot about the white man camped next to us.

Henry Johnson: I could hear Melissa setting the table and could smell the pie baking as I pulled Bessie-Belle up to the house. By evening time I'm usually as hungry as a bear, but my concern about the Indians took away my appetite. I picked at my supper, my eyes never straying from the big gun leaning beside the door and the powder horn hanging from the peg. I didn't touch the pie, just grabbed the gun and told Melissa I was stepping out to smoke a pipe.

Melissa Johnson: The pie was better than I expected. I ate Henry's piece, too! The baby was fussing, so I quickly cleaned off the table and stuffed the tin plates and utensils into the burlap bag. I planned to take them down to the stream for cleaning later. I fed the baby and he fell right to sleep.

Wild Tooth: I couldn't eat much. The rabbit was tender, but my thoughts never strayed from the white man and his gun. The old women began to sing moon chants, and the kids chased the dogs. Rather than joining in the storytelling, I grabbed my bow and quiver and moved off toward the trees to stand guard. I didn't like living this way. I would have preferred to be on horseback running deer or hunting buffalo.

Talking Feather: I fed the bones to the dogs. Watching the children chase the dogs made me laugh. As the old women sang moon chants, I slipped from the fire circle and moved across the meadow toward the stream. The water was still cold from the mountain snow, but I wanted to wash the dust of the journey from my hair.

Melissa Johnson: I had forgotten about the Indians. Like I always do after supper, I grabbed the bag of dishes and slipped outside. I left the sleeping baby in the cabin. I couldn't see Henry, but I could see the glow of his pipe near a small stand of trees. My bag softly rattled as I headed for the stream to wash the dishes.

Narrator 1: It was a night of the full Moon. Silver and bright, the Moon lifted from the horizon and bathed the big sky Montana territories in its crystal light.

Talking Feather: I had washed my hair and was rubbing it with sweet herbs when I saw her. She was on the other side of the stream, rinsing something in the water. We looked at each other as the Moon skipped across the water like a shiny stone. If her skin hadn't been so pale, she would have looked like an Indian maiden. She would have looked somewhat like me.

Narrator 2: The Moon illuminated the two women as they went about daily routines common to both.

Melissa Johnson: I was about half done with the wash when I saw the Indian woman across the stream. She was rubbing leaves through her wet hair. It was a moment frozen in time; neither of us moved, and I could hardly breathe. In a few seconds, I settled down and looked at her, studying this unfamiliar person. She was pretty and looked my age. In fact, she looked a lot like me.

Narrator 1: It seemed as if the women had discovered that they were not so different after all. But it would remain to be seen if the husbands could share that same discovery.

Henry Johnson: I came in from smoking my pipe and discovered Melissa was gone. I grabbed my gun and raced down the path toward the stream. My heart was pounding and my head was filled with frightening images. I found Melissa at the edge of the stream. Just across the water was an Indian woman who looked much like her. I grabbed Melissa's arm in an effort to lead her back to the cabin.

Narrator 2: If the women had discovered that they need not fear each other, certainly their husbands had not.

Henry Johnson: But she resisted. With a smile on her face, she gently rose and started walking slowly. She glanced back across the stream and let her gaze linger on the Indian.

Wild Tooth: When I realized that Talking Feather was not in camp, I raced to the stream. My fingers were wrapped around the handle of my knife. I saw her at the edge of the water, gazing at a woman on the other side. Talking Feather didn't move. She was staring at the white woman. A slight smile appeared on her lips. I grabbed her arm and tried to pull her up and back toward camp. At first she resisted, but then she rose and began to walk with me. She glanced back across the stream and let her gaze linger on the white woman.

Narrator: As dawn broke the next morning, Henry was surprised to see that the Indians had broken camp, leaving few signs that they had ever been there. He and Melissa went about their daily routine. Melissa seemed thoughtful, but happy. The Indians did not return. But as they traveled from one campsite to another, Talking Feather could often be seen gazing across a stream with a small smile on her face.

The End